Hi, friend! I'm Max. Stick around to read my story, meet my friends, and learn about the beauty of neurodiversity along the way. I'm so happy you're here!

We all think differently

We all think differently

We all think differently

We all think differently

We all think differently

We all think differently

We all think differently

We all think differently

We all think differently

We all think differently

We all think differently

We all think differently

We all think differently

We all think differently

We all think differently

We all think differently

We all think differently

We all think differently

# MAX
## AND THE TOWER OF ACCEPTANCE

*Alyssa Lego*

**Story Arc Books**
Toms River, NJ

Published by
Story Arc Books | Toms River, NJ

Publisher's Cataloging-in-Publication Data Lego, Alyssa.
Title: subtitle / Alyssa Lego. – Toms River, NJ : Story Arc Books, 2023.
p. ; cm.
979-8-3979100-8-8 (print SC)
Children—Case studies. 2. Mission-focused—Autism Appreciation
Rainbow heart infinity symbol designed by Linda McCauley; reprinted with permission.
Printed in the United States of America

# DEDICATION

To my beautiful brother, Michael:

You are my constant source of inspiration, and your unique way of experiencing the world has forever shaped my perspective. In your gentle presence, I have learned the true meaning of acceptance, empathy, and the beauty of neurodiversity.

This book is a celebration of your light, a tribute to the countless smiles you've brought to our lives, and a testament to the incredible journey we've embarked on together. With every turn of the page, may it spread love, understanding, and acceptance to children far and wide, helping them embrace the wonderful tapestry of differences that make us who we are.

Thank you, Michael, for being my guiding star and teaching me the true meaning of unconditional love. Your spirit will forever shine through these words, igniting a beacon of hope for all who read them.

Once upon a time, there was a school filled with children of all different shapes, sizes, colors, and personalities. They laughed, played, and learned together every day. But there was one child who seemed a bit different from the rest. His name was Max. Max was autistic.

Max played by himself, flapping his hands and spinning in circles. He didn't always know how to join in with the other kids' games or understand their jokes. Sometimes, they even laughed at him and called him names, which made him feel sad, confused, and alone.

One day, a new teacher named Ms. Jones arrived at the school. She noticed how the other children treated Max and knew that she had to do something to help them understand him better. She began by teaching the class about neurodiversity. Neurodiversity means that everyone's brain works differently, and that's okay.

Ms. Jones explained that some people have autism or other differences that affect the way they learn, communicate, or behave. But that doesn't make them less valuable or important than anyone else. Their unique skills can help us all learn and grow.

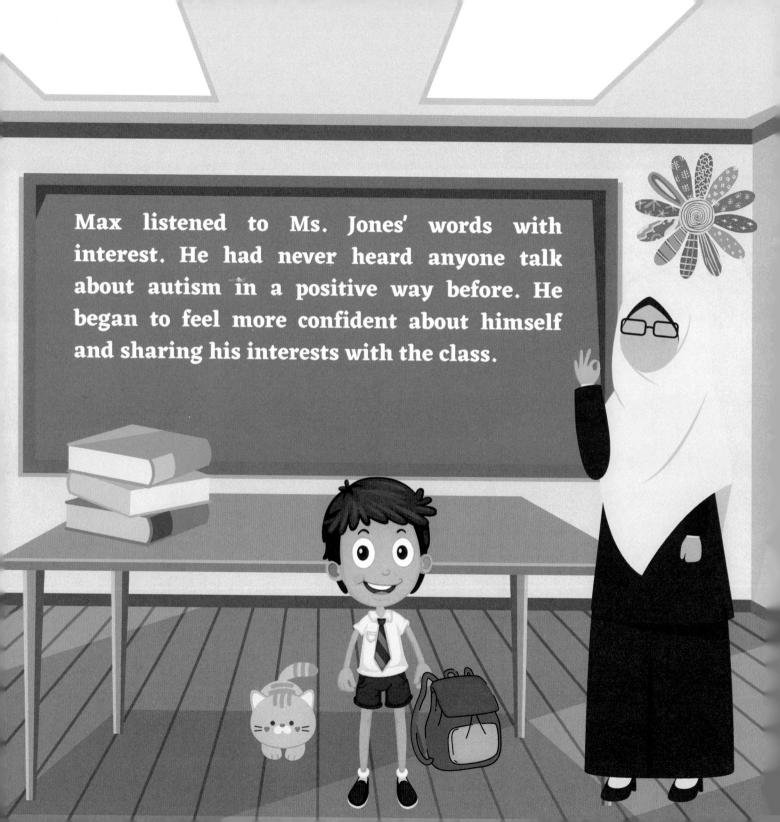

Max listened to Ms. Jones' words with interest. He had never heard anyone talk about autism in a positive way before. He began to feel more confident about himself and sharing his interests with the class.

One day, the class had a science project where they had to build a tower out of blocks. Max had always loved building things, so he was excited to try. But when he started to stack the blocks, he became so focused that he didn't notice when some of the other kids knocked it over by accident.

Max felt frustrated and upset. He thought they were trying to ruin his tower on purpose. But then, Ms. Jones helped everyone understand what had happened. She told them that, just because Max's brain worked differently than theirs, it didn't mean that they couldn't be friends. Ms. Jones had the class rebuild Max's tower together.

The students began to see Max in a new way. They no longer laughed at him or called him names. Instead, they began to embrace his unique mind.

Max became a valued member of the class, and he continued to share his interests and passions with his friends. The other children also began to open up about their own differences and unique qualities, creating a culture of acceptance and understanding throughout the school.

We all think differently

The summer came and the students went to different classes in the fall. But they never forgot the lessons they learned from Ms. Jones and Max. They carried the message of neurodiversity and acceptance with them throughout their lives, making the world a more inclusive and compassionate place for all.

And Max, who once felt like an outsider, became a leader and advocate for himself and his other neurodivergent friends. He continued to build his own masterpieces, each one a testament to the power of embracing neurodiversity and celebrating individuality.

The End

"Thank you for reading my story. Remember to treat all of your friends - and the friends you have not met yet - with kindness and respect. Stay connected with us to hear the story of my friend, Lily!

# ABOUT
# YOU, ME, NEURODIVERSITY

Introducing "You, Me, Neurodiversity" - a new children's book series dedicated to fostering autism acceptance and promoting understanding of neurodiversity among young readers. With a mission to combat ableism and create a more inclusive society, these engaging and age-appropriate stories take children on inspiring adventures, teaching them the beauty of friendship and embracing differences along the way.

Follow along as our endearing characters navigate everyday challenges, highlighting the strengths and unique perspectives of individuals on the autism spectrum. Each book in the series captivates young minds and serves as a powerful tool for sparking meaningful conversations about acceptance, empathy, and friendship.

What makes You, Me, Neurodiversity even more special is that every purchase supports charitable organizations dedicated to supporting the autistic community. By immersing yourself and your child or student in these meaningful stories, you're not only enriching their imaginations but also making a positive impact on the lives of others.

Join us on this journey of understanding, compassion, and respect. Let's inspire the next generation to embrace neurodiversity, celebrate differences, and build a world free from prejudice and ableism. Together, we can create a brighter future for all - one character at a time.

# ABOUT THE AUTHOR

Alyssa Lego is a young prolific writer, thought leader, and philanthropist.

At the age of fourteen, she co-founded the Morgan Marie Michael Foundation after witnessing the ableism that her younger brother, Michael, faced and felt compelled to act. An engaging communicator, Lego made her book debut with a memoir in 2020 and is thrilled to introduce Max and the Tower of Acceptance as the first installment in her new children's book series, You, Me, Neurodiversity. Dedicated to enhancing the lives of autistic individuals, particularly adults, Lego donates book royalties to charitable organizations that serve the autistic community.

Lego is a rising junior at Boston College, who hopes to channel her love for writing, speaking, and connecting with others into a career in strategic communications and public relations.

We all think differently

We all think differently

We all think differently

We all think differently

We all think differently

We all think differently

We all think differently

We all think differently

We all think differently

We all think differently

We all think differently

We all think differently

We all think differently

We all think differently

We all think differently

We all think differently

We all think differently

We all think differently

We all think differently

We all think differently

We all think differently

We all think differently

We all think differently

We all think differently

We all think differently

We all think differently

We all think differently

Made in the USA
Middletown, DE
09 October 2023